W9-AHH-288

From anonomouse

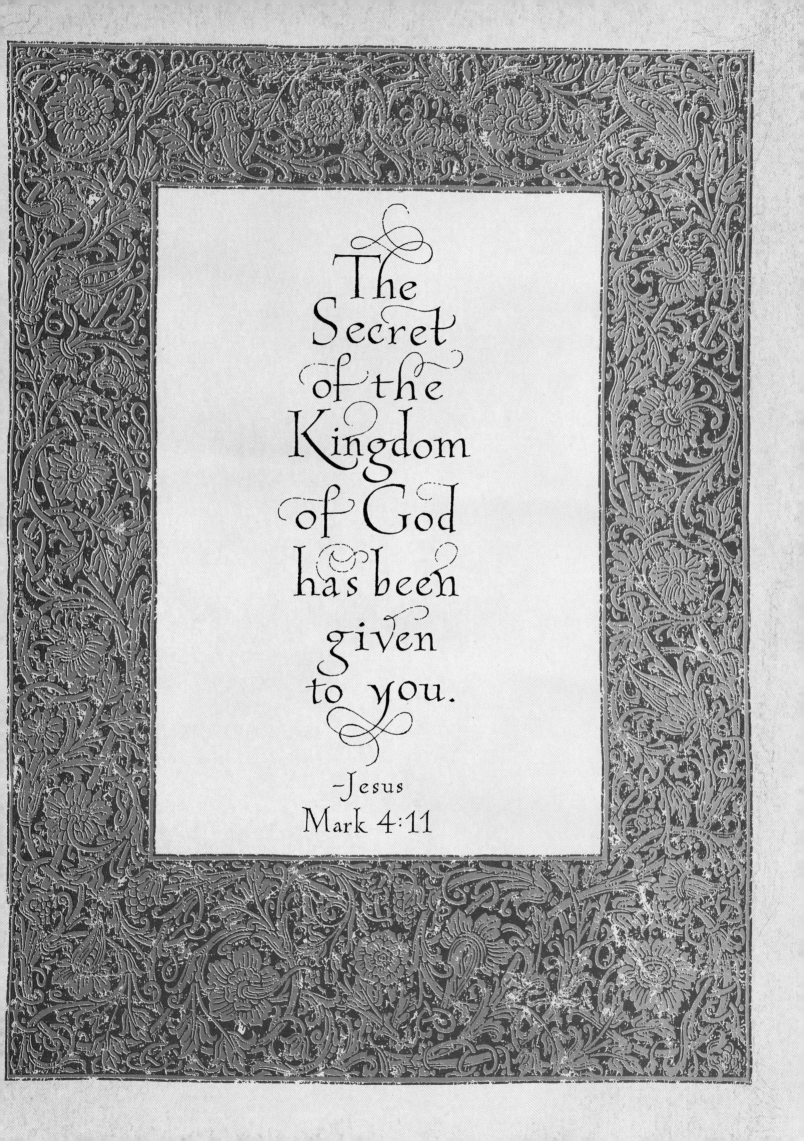

The
Secret
of the
Kingdom
of God
has been
given
to you.

–Jesus
Mark 4:11

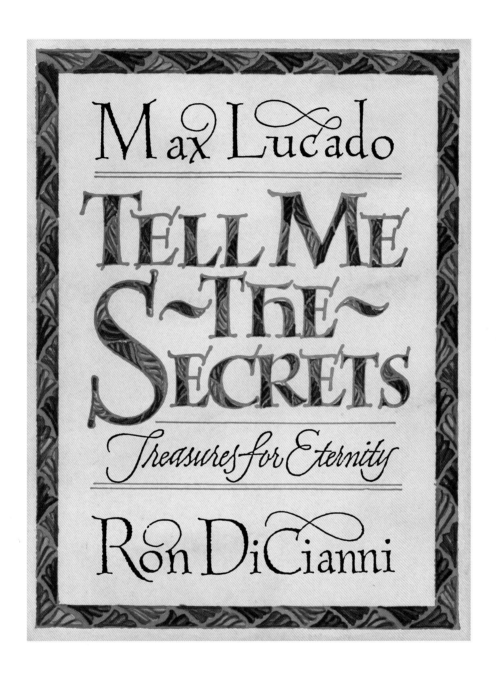

Max Lucado

TELL ME ~THE~ SECRETS

Treasures for Eternity

Ron DiCianni

CROSSWAY BOOKS • WHEATON, ILLINOIS
A DIVISION OF GOOD NEWS PUBLISHERS

ACKNOWLEDGMENTS

Thanks, Pat, for putting up with my personality. I know how much you do to allow me the freedom to work.
Grant and Warren, *you* are the reason I undertook this project.
Pastor Maddox, thanks for the direction.
Max, I am in your debt.
Lane, Brian, and Mark, thanks for not failing at the finish line. I knew you wouldn't.
Most of all, thanks to the Master who gave us the "secrets" so they wouldn't be secret any longer.

—RON DiCIANNI

Special thanks to Lane Dennis and Ron DiCianni for convincing me this project was needed. Appreciation to Steve Green, Karen Hill, and Lila Bishop for watching the wording in contract and manuscript. And a special word for my three daughters: Jenna, Andrea, and Sara for telling me secrets of life over and over again.

—MAX LUCADO

Tell Me the Secrets.

Copyright © 1993 by Max Lucado.

Published by Crossway Books
        a division of Good News Publishers
        1300 Crescent Street
        Wheaton, Illinois 60187.

All rights reserved. No part of this publication may be reproduced, stored in a retrieval system or transmitted in any form by any means, electronic, mechanical, photocopy, recording, or otherwise, without the prior permission of the publisher, except as provided by USA copyright law.

Illustrations: Ron DiCianni

Cover design: The Puckett Group

Calligraphy: Joey Hannaford

Art Direction/Design: Mark Schramm

First printing 1993

Printed in the United States of America

Unless otherwise marked, Scripture verses are taken from *The Holy Bible, New Century Version,* copyright © 1987, 1988, 1991 by Word Publishing, Dallas, TX 75039. Used by permission.

Scripture verses marked NIV are taken from the *Holy Bible: New International Version*®. Copyright © 1973, 1978, 1984 by International Bible Society. Used by permission of Zondervan Publishing House. All rights reserved.

The "NIV" and "New International Version" trademarks are registered in the United States Patent and Trademark Office by International Bible Society. Use of either trademark requires the permission of International Bible Society.

Verses marked TLB are taken from *The Living Bible* © 1971. Used by permission of Tyndale House Publishers, Inc., Wheaton, IL 60189. All rights reserved.

Library of Congress Cataloging-in-Publication Data
Lucado, Max.
    Tell me the secrets / written by Max Lucado ; illustrations by Ron
DiCianni ; calligraphy by Joey Hannaford.
      p.   cm.
    1. Christian fiction, American. I. DiCianni, Ron. II. Title.
PS3562.U225T45 1993   813'.54—dc20   93-25957
ISBN 0-89107-730-8

01		00		99		98		97		96		95		94	
15	14	13	12	11	10	9	8	7	6	5	4	3	2	

FROM THE AUTHOR

Dedicated to
Zachary and Jared

FROM THE ARTIST

To
Grant and Warren
Never forget . . .

—Dad

To Parents

DEAR PARENT:

Before you open this book, be advised. The perspective of your children is about to be forever altered—if you *choose* it to be, that is. What we've done in the pages of this book is merely a beginning. The ending is in your hands, right where it belongs. If the experts are correct, your children are right now deciding their values for life. If you end the reading sessions in this book by saying, "Okay, time for bed," you will have missed the opportunity to mold those values.

Consider every chapter of this book a launch pad. Be creative. Innovative. But most of all, *impassioned.* Let your children know what you really believe. Allow them to tell you what they really think about each concept. Dialogue. Imagine with them what might happen if you dare employ these "secrets" in your lives. Remind each other often by doing a "secret check." Then get ready for the blessing of God.

Don't give up. God knows your very names. Psalm 4:3 (NIV) says, "Know that the Lord has set apart the godly for himself." Could this be referring to you and your family?

—MAX AND RON

The Shadow House

The Lord tells his secrets to
those who respect him.

PSALM 25:14

T FIRST LANDON thought he could catch the baseball before it hit the ground, but after a few steps he knew there was no way. Eric had slammed it high into the sky—higher than any of them had ever hit a ball before. Landon just stopped and stared as the ball crashed through the window of the house all the kids feared—the Shadow House.

No one he knew ever went near the place. Kids said that some people saw lights in the house at night. No one knew for sure. No one knew because no one got close. It loomed at the end of the street like a haunted castle.

Eric caught up with Landon and stood beside him. "Where'd the ball go?" he panted.

Landon pointed at a broken window on the second floor. Somewhere behind it, on a dusty floor littered with broken glass, was the baseball. Landon's baseball. His brand new baseball. The ball his dad caught last week at a pro game.

He couldn't go home without it.

The boys stared at the old house. It was eerie. Tall oak trees. Gray, peeling paint. Loose shingles. Dangling shutters. A disconnected drainage pipe leaned outward. Some

9

windows were cracked and others boarded shut. The waist-high picket fence was nearly buried in the tall grass and weeds.

"We're in big trouble now." The voice was Shannon's, Landon's little sister.

She was only nine but could throw a strong fastball and had a good glove, so Eric and Landon always included her when they played. Besides, there weren't too many kids in the neighborhood. Most families with children lived out in the suburbs. But Eric and Landon lived in the center of town—an old section with old houses. Some pretty. Some scary—like the Shadow House.

"Wow," Eric sighed, staring at the broken window. "That would've been out of the park at Jersen's field."

"Yeah, but this isn't Jersen's field and you're not in a game. This is the Shadow House, and you're in deep trouble."

Landon and Eric were both twelve, but their age was the only thing they had in common. Eric was tall and athletic. Landon was short and skinny. Eric always wore a baseball hat and carried his glove. Landon wore glasses and carried a book.

If there had been more kids in the neighborhood, the two might never have met. But since there weren't, Eric and Landon were stuck with each other. Over the years they'd become friends. The friendship had helped them both. Eric had learned how to run a computer, and Landon had learned where to buy baseball cards at the mall—a place both would rather have been at this moment.

"Someone has to go up there," Shannon said, knowing that out of the three it wouldn't be her.

"What if we just forget the ball?" Eric asked.

"We can't do that. It's a new ball. Besides we broke a window. We've got to . . . we've got to go up there and get it."

"We?" Eric and Shannon questioned at the same time.

"Yes, we," Landon explained. "Shannon threw it, and Eric hit it, and I'm the oldest."

Landon was only two months older than Eric. But it was enough to make him feel important, especially since he was the shorter of the two. This time Eric didn't mind the reminder.

"Well, since you are older, you go by yourself."

"No way, Eric. We're all going."

Landon looked up at Eric and down at Shannon. Then Shannon and Eric looked at each other. "All right," they groaned.

The wooden gate of the picket fence creaked as Landon pulled it open. The three gulped and stepped into the yard of the Shadow House.

Porch boards groaned beneath their feet as they approached the door. "Hope the door is unlocked," Shannon said.

"Shhh," cautioned the boys. They hoped it wasn't.

It was. The screen door creaked, the iron doorknob squeaked, and a musty smell met Landon as he opened the door. He looked back at the others and then stepped inside.

A shaft of light from a side window fell across sheet-draped furniture and landed at the base of a large stone hearth. Three sets of wide eyes peered into the semidarkness.

"Is it vacant?" Eric whispered.

"I certainly hope so," Landon answered.

"Look, here is a kitchen," Shannon said aloud.

"Shhh," the boys responded.

She didn't hear them. She was already inside, staring at the large cabinets and high ceilings. "Wow, this place is old."

"Shannon, come back," Landon whispered as loudly as he could. He was still near the entryway. "Let's come back later with Dad." He was just about to tell Eric to go get Shannon when he saw a hat and jacket hanging on the wall by the kitchen door. Neither was dusty. The house was old, but the hat and coat weren't. He swallowed hard. "S-S-Somebody is here," he said in a low voice.

But no one heard him. Shannon was still in the kitchen, and Eric was . . . Eric was . . . *Eric? Eric?* "Oh boy. Eric's gone!"

His thoughts began to race. *I'll run home. No, I can't abandon Eric and Shannon. I'll scream. No, that would only tell the hat-and-coat man we're here. I could . . . I could . . .* But he couldn't think of another idea.

He didn't have to.

Suddenly a hand was on his shoulder. He whirled around. Sunlight from the doorway washed over the back of the man. His features were hidden in the shadow, but his size wasn't. He was big—big and tall—and his hand was huge. And his hand was still on Landon's shoulder.

His other hand was tossing a ball in the air. "Looking for this?"

Before Landon could answer, Eric's voice came from another room. "Landon, come here! It's awesome! Shields and spears and knives. Come and see."

Landon looked back up at the man. "Uh, we were just playing ball. We didn't mean to break . . ."

Then another voice entered the room. It was Shannon's. "Hey, guys, there's soda in the fridge. Somebody must be here."

"Looks like you've made yourselves at home," the stranger's voice boomed in the half-empty parlor.

Landon looked up at the face, still shadowed. He could see a heavy moustache and the shape of a strong jaw. "Let's see what your friends have found," it said. Landon's stomach tightened as the strong hand guided him across the room.

Through the doorway he could see Eric on his knees beside an old chest, his back to Landon.

"Eric," Landon said softly.

Eric didn't look up. "Check it out, Landon! This chest is full of neat stuff. Beads and coins and—wow, here is a headdress with feathers and—" Eric turned to show his find and then stopped at what he saw.

The man behind Landon was snowy-haired and had bushy eyebrows. He wore a plaid shirt, blue overalls, work boots, and . . . a big smile.

"It's all real," the older man explained. "All from the heart of Africa. Melva, come in here. Looks like our neighbors have come to meet us."

A small lady with gray hair tucked under a baseball hat appeared from the other room and smiled. "I've already met one of them." Beside her stood Shannon, beaming and drinking a root beer.

"You must be Grandpa Josh," Shannon said. "Melva told me your name."

The old man's eyebrows lifted in delight. "That's who I am. We've just returned from Africa. People call us retired missionaries. But there's no such thing. We're all missionaries, and we never retire. It's just that some of us go overseas and some have to come home when they get too old."

He winked at Shannon. "That's me."

"How old are you?" she asked.

"Old enough to know what matters and what doesn't," he riddled, "and old enough to know a few secrets. Here, sit down and tell me about yourselves."

It suddenly occurred to Landon that he was the only nervous one in the room and that he didn't have to be. He let out a sigh and took a seat on a big stuffed couch.

"Bought this old house in an auction," Josh explained. "We don't have much money, but we do have time, so we're gonna fix her up."

"Where'd you get all this stuff?" Eric asked, walking back to the wooden chest.

"Collected it through the years when we were in African countries teaching tribes-people about God. Go ahead and look."

Eric didn't have to be told twice. He carefully pulled out more relics: a purple robe, a gold sash, an ivory bracelet. "It goes on the ankle," Josh explained.

Landon joined Eric at the chest and lifted out a bag of coins. "Those aren't used anymore. An old man gave them to me. A Dutch trader had given them to him years ago."

As the boys gathered around Josh and looked at the gold, Shannon took her turn at the chest. She reached inside and pulled out a cloth bag closed at the top with a drawstring. Out of the bag she pulled a book. The leather binding was soft. A strap locked it.

"You'll need a key to open it."

Shannon hadn't realized Josh was looking.

"The key is around my neck," he explained patting his chest.

"What kind of book is it?"

"It's my most valuable treasure. It's a book of secrets."

"A book of what?" Eric inquired.

"Secrets. Secrets learned in a life well lived."

"What kind of secrets?" Landon asked looking over Shannon's shoulder.

"Secrets of life."

The kids looked up with confused expressions, so Josh explained.

"There are secrets to living well. This book contains the lessons learned by a man who sought the secrets of life."

"Did he find them?"

"Some of them."

"What are they?"

A big smile spread beneath the long moustache. "Ahhh, that's the first secret. You only hear them when you ask the question."

"What question?"

Josh's eyes twinkled. "I'll know when I hear it, and you'll know when you ask it, and when we know, I'll open the book. But till then, we've got another matter to discuss." He rolled the baseball in his big hands.

"We're really sorry about the window," Landon volunteered.

"Well, I'm glad you are. What do you think we ought to do about it?"

"Learn from the mistake?" Eric asked. Landon elbowed him.

But Josh smiled. "That's one thing we'll do," he assured.

"We don't have much money," Landon explained. "Only $3.19 between all of us."

"Not enough to repair a window, eh?" Josh replied. "But I have an idea. This house needs a lot of work. What if I hire the three of you to clean up my yard in exchange for the window?"

"It needs a lot of work," Shannon said.

"Well, it's either that, or you could see if your parents could loan you the money."

"We'll handle the grass," Eric said quickly.

"Great! After you finish your drinks, I'll show you the tools."

And so began the friendship with Josh and Melva, the missionaries who would teach Eric, Landon, and Shannon the secrets of life.

The Secret of
FORGIVENESS

Get along with each other,
and forgive each other.

COLOSSIANS 3:13

RANDPA JOSH could tell something was bothering Shannon by the way she walked onto the porch.

For the last month she'd stopped by every afternoon on her way home from school. She would bound up the steps and run in the door without even knocking, knowing Melva would have some cookies and Josh would have a story or a song.

Since she loved stories, cookies, and songs, she was always dropping in for a visit. But today not even all three would help.

"Why the sad face, Shannon?" Josh asked as he met her at the door.

Shannon's brown eyes were filled with tears, and her round cheeks were streaked. "It's Jessica."

"The girl who sits next to you in class?"

"Yeah."

"What happened?"

"She made fun of me all day. Somehow she found out that my parents are divorced, and she started calling me 'Little Orphan Shannie.' Why would she do that, Grandpa Josh? I didn't make my parents fight. It's not my fault. And I'm not an orphan."

Forgiven

"Of course you aren't," Grandpa Josh assured her. "Come on in. Let's talk about it."

"How could she say those things to me?" Shannon blurted as they walked through the door. "She got all the girls in class to stand around me and call me names. I never did anything to her. In fact, I even help her with fractions. She stinks at math, and I help her a lot. Now I think she stinks at more than math."

Josh stopped and looked down at his little friend. He put his hand under her chin, lifted her face, and said, "I think it's time to share a secret with you, Shannon. Let's skip the cookies for now. Follow me."

The two stepped into the room where Eric had first discovered the chest. It was neat now. Melva and Josh had turned it into a little museum. The walls were covered with photos and paintings. Weapons of the bushmen stood in the corner, and on the table in front of the couch lay two books. One was a well-worn Bible, and the other was the leather book of secrets.

Josh picked it up.

"It's not very thick," Shannon observed.

"Doesn't have to be. True wisdom is shared simply."

Josh handed the book to Shannon. She opened it and read the words written by hand, "Secrets of Life."

"Secrets. Each secret with a message. Why don't I read you the first one?"

"What's it about?"

"It's about something you need to give Jessica."

"A lecture?"

"No." Josh smiled.

Grandpa Josh reached into the bib of his overalls and pulled out his glasses. "Have a seat, Shannon. Let me read you the story."

So as the two sat in the square of sunlight left by the open window, Josh began to read.

The Watermaster

Years ago there was a village in a desert. Water was scarce, and the people treasured what little they had. It seldom rained, but when it did, people scurried about to capture it in buckets and pots. Every drop was a treasure. Every cup was precious.

For that reason the discovery in the cavern was thrilling news.

One day a farmer was digging holes for fence posts. A few feet below the surface of the ground he found a cavern—not large, but full of water.

He immediately lowered a bucket, pulled it out, and tasted, to his delight, cold, sweet water. He was so excited he filled all his buckets, loaded them in the back of his wagon, and hurried into the village.

"I have water! I have water!" he shouted. The villagers came running out of their houses. As the people gathered, the farmer explained how he had come upon the treasure. He joyfully announced that there was enough for everyone. "Drink all you want," he offered. And then, to the people's amazement, he picked up a bucket and doused a little boy.

"There is plenty!" he proclaimed. "Enjoy it." And with that the people began to laugh and splash each other. For the first time as long as anyone could remember, there was enough water for everyone.

After the celebration, the farmer announced his plan. "I'll bring some water in every morning so each of you can have what you need."

And that's exactly what he did. The farmer became the watermaster. Every morning he loaded the buckets into his wagon, rode into town, and gave some water to the people. It was a new day. The water was free. The farmer was willing, and the villagers were grateful.

Until one night when the farmer had a dream.

In the dream he saw the people taking the water and not being thankful. They would walk up to the wagon, snatch the bucket, and march away without a word of appreciation.

When he awoke, he was troubled. As he rode into town, he resolved to give the water only to the grateful.

Before he allowed the people to take their buckets, he announced, "From now on, I will not give water to those who aren't thankful." The people were surprised. Each person thanked him when he or she received the water.

All was well until the farmer had another dream. In this dream some of the people who were drinking the water were unkind to their neighbors and mean to their animals. The next morning he was bothered again. He decided he would only give the water to worthy individuals.

"If you are mean to your animals or unkind to your neighbors, you will get no water," he decreed.

The people looked at each other and were silent. They knew the bad people among them. When the watermaster saw the looks of distrust, he had an idea.

"Each of you come and tell me who is unworthy so I will know who is mean and unkind."

So one by one they came with their names, and he made a list. The list grew and grew. Finally, after every villager had spoken, the farmer read the names. He was shocked. Every person in the town was on the list except one.

The farmer.

So he stood on the wagon and announced that since few were grateful and none were worthy, he would bring no more water to the village. And he turned his wagon of water around and went home.

✧✧✧

Grandpa Josh looked up from the book at Shannon. Her brow was knitted in anger.

"That's not right," she protested. "He can't do that. Who is he to decide who gets water and who doesn't?"

"What do you mean?"

"Well, it wasn't his water to begin with. It was a gift. His job was to give it to everyone, not just to those who were thankful and good."

"You think it's wrong to keep something good from a bad person?"

"Well, yeah. I mean, look at Jesus. He gave good things to bad people all the time. Remember the time He healed those lepers who didn't say thanks?"

"I'm glad you mentioned Jesus, Shannon. A verse from the Bible is quoted at the end of this story. It's something Jesus said. Want to read it?"

He handed Shannon the book, and she read the words:

"Love your enemies! Do good to them! Lend to them! . . . and you will be truly acting as sons of God: for he is kind to the unthankful and to those who are very wicked." (Luke 6:35 TLB)

Shannon looked up quickly. "That's exactly what I mean. Just because someone is mean, you can't be mean to them. If you are then, well, then you'll be just as mean as they—"

She stopped. Her face softened into a slow smile.

"Jessica?"

"Yes. Jessica," Josh replied.

"She's been mean."

"She sure has. But God has been good. As long as you live, Shannon, you will meet people like Jessica. You can't avoid them. But you can go deep into the water of love that God has given you. And He will help you forgive."

"That's the secret?"

"That's the secret. Look it's written below the verse at the bottom of the page."

Shannon read the words slowly.

"Be quick to share the water of grace with your enemies—as a gift for them, just as it was a gift to you."

Forgiveness

Funny how often when we think we are hurting the other guy, we really wind up self-destructing. We writhe in agony over a wrong done to us, and we think that the other party is feeling the same intense anger and pain—to say nothing of what we are feeling when we plot revenge. In truth, the other party usually doesn't feel a thing, and we only injure ourselves. No wonder Jesus commanded us to forgive and to put the matter into His hands for the proper doling out of justice and mercy. Consider this: Did you receive what you deserve from God? I didn't. He chose to forgive me. And you.

Besides, if you allow the "wrong" to eat away at you, you're actually letting the other person continue to hurt you. As always God takes the higher road. Decide to follow His footsteps. They lead home.

✧✧✧

"For if you forgive men when they sin against you, your heavenly Father will also forgive you." MATTHEW 6:14 (NIV)

" . . . forgive, and you will be forgiven." LUKE 6:37 (NIV)

"Forgive us our sins, for we also forgive everyone who sins against us." LUKE 11:4 (NIV)

"Bear with each other and forgive whatever grievances you may have against one another. Forgive as the Lord forgave you." COLOSSIANS 3:13 (NIV)

The Secret of
PEACE

We set our eyes not on what we see,
but on what we cannot see.
What we see will last only a short time.
But what we cannot see will last forever.

2 CORINTHIANS 4:18

JOSH WATCHED Eric get up from the table, walk across the room, and stand by the kitchen window. "I don't understand it, Grandpa Josh. All I did was stand up for my beliefs."

Rain streaked the pane. Josh stirred his coffee. Eric stared out the window. Both were silent—Eric wondering why the kids laughed at him, Josh wondering what he should say.

"I'm not the only Christian in science class." Eric broke the silence. "Why didn't anyone else speak up?"

"Tell me again what the teacher said."

Eric looked at Josh and let out a sigh. "He said I should know better than to believe in God."

"And the students laughed?"

"Yeah, they laughed. They laugh at anything he says. You've got to understand—this teacher is a class act. He's young. He's sharp. The girls think he's handsome. We're not talking old fogey here. We're talking about the most popular teacher in school."

"Did any student speak up?"

Peace

"Not for God. I guess they didn't want to look foolish." Eric turned again and looked out the window. "I guess they didn't want to look like me. What bothers me most is not the silence of the kids but the silence of God."

"What do you mean?" Josh asked.

"Why didn't He do something? Why did He let everyone laugh at me? Why didn't He zap the teacher or shake the room?"

"How do you know He didn't?"

"'Cause I was there. When the teacher asked who believed in God, I raised my hand. He said I was foolish, and everybody laughed. He lectured for ten minutes on how faith was old-fashioned. I didn't see God do anything. Not one thing!"

Josh stroked his long moustache and smiled. "You know, Eric, you aren't the first one to ask that question."

"What do you mean?"

"Go to a hospital. Walk up and down the halls, and you'll find people asking the same thing, 'Why doesn't God do something?' Go where hungry people are. They'll ask it, too. 'If God is alive, why doesn't He help?' You're not the first one to question the presence of God."

Josh stood up and motioned. "Follow me. I want to show you something."

The two stepped into the study where Josh kept his treasure chest from Africa. Josh led Eric to a table in the corner.

"Have I shown you my pets?" he asked, pointing to a glass cage. Inside the cage four little mice huddled in a corner.

"When did you get these?"

"Melva bought them last week at the pet store. She loves animals. Here, meet Ezrod." Josh reached into the cage and lifted out the smallest of the mice. He was snow white with a nose that never stopped wiggling.

"He was born here. Right in this room."

Eric was puzzled. *What does a mouse have to do with looking stupid in science class?*

"Ezrod has something to teach you about peace, Eric," Josh explained as he put the rodent in Eric's hands.

"What?"

"This mouse knows how you feel."

Eric turned Ezrod around and looked at his small, whiskered face. "I don't get it."

"Well, Ezrod has questions, too."

Eric rolled his eyes. "Right. Like what?"

"Like the other day he complained about the monsters on the wall."

"Come on." Eric chuckled.

"No really. See the framed photograph?"

"That's you and Melva."

"Ezrod doesn't think so. He's convinced that it's a window with two monsters staring in, waiting for a chance to eat him."

"Josh, you're crazy." Eric was starting to laugh.

Josh's eyes twinkled. "And that's just the beginning. See the walking stick in the corner?"

"Yeah."

"Ezrod thinks it's a snake."

"You're kidding. It doesn't look anything like a snake."

"Ezrod doesn't know that. You know what else he complains about?"

"What?"

"He complains that I leave him alone in the room too much. He thinks if he can't see me, then I'm not alive. If he had his way, I'd be here in this room twenty-four hours a day."

"Wait a second. You're telling me that you have a mouse who thinks the picture is a monster, that a stick is a snake, and that if he can't see you, then you don't exist?"

"That's right."

"That's insane."

"No, that's life through the eyes of a mouse. And you know, Eric, I can understand his confusion. You see, Ezrod has no knowledge of life beyond this room. His entire world is right here. The ceiling is the sky. The walls are the edge of the earth. All he knows is this room."

Eric leaned forward on the couch and stroked the back of the mouse. He was starting to get the point. "Ezrod doesn't understand that the real world is bigger than what he can see," he said slowly.

"That's right. He misinterprets what he *can* see and doesn't understand what he *can't* see."

"Kind of like me."

"Kind of like all of us. We all forget that God's world is much bigger than ours. From God's point of view, this earth is just one room in a huge house. We can only see a portion of what exists."

Eric nodded his head. "And since our vision is limited, we think pictures are monsters. We think sticks are snakes. And we think if we don't see the owner of the house, he isn't here."

"That's right. Let me show you something."

Josh went to the shelf and took down the book of secrets, opened it, and handed it to Eric.

"Read the verse on this page."

Eric read the words slowly:

"We set our eyes not on what we see, but on what we cannot see. What we see will last only a short time. But what we cannot see will last forever." (2 Corinthians 4:18)

"What does it mean to set your eyes on what you cannot see?" Eric asked.

"Ah, good question. I learned what this meant in jail."

Eric's eyes widened. "You did?"

"I was working near a small village in the jungle. We dug water wells for the people. We became their friends and told them about God. They were interested, but the chief was angry. He had me thrown into a hut and locked the door."

"What happened?"

"Well, while I was locked up, I asked the same questions you asked. I hadn't done anything wrong. I began to wonder where God was. As the days passed, I became anxious. Then I remembered this verse in the Bible. 'We set our eyes not on what we see, but on what we cannot see.'

"So I decided to do it. I decided to see with my heart and not my eyes. They could lock up my body, but they couldn't lock my heart. I spent hours sitting on the dirt floor of that hut talking to God and soaring with him like an eagle through the sky. I was a prisoner, but my spirit was free."

Eric was fascinated. "How long were you locked up?"

"Thirty days. I later learned that they were just testing me to see if I was serious about my faith."

"Have they become Christians?"

"Not yet. But they may. At least they saw one person who was willing to stand up for his belief."

"Do you think my teacher was just testing me?"

"Could be. Could be he isn't, though. Your teacher may mock you every day from now on. Your friends may laugh at you. But when they do, see the unseen. God is near. He is proud of you, Eric. He loves those who are loyal to Him. And just because He doesn't make the ceiling fall or the ground shake, that doesn't mean He isn't by your side."

Eric was quiet for a minute. Then he smiled. "I guess Ezrod and I have a lot in common."

"What do you mean?"

"We both just need to trust. We both need to see more than we can see. And we both have you to remind us there is more to this world than what we can see."

Peace

Over the years I have often heard people say things such as, "I'm happy in the Lord." They probably mean that at that particular time everything in their lives is going well. The family is healthy, the job is okay, they got the new car, and they have a few dollars to put away. But what happens if God allows one of those things to change?

I've often wondered how Peter and Paul sang in prison. Beats me. I once heard that peace is not the absence of storms in our lives. Peace is what you get *in* the storm. Too many times I haven't allowed God to give me His peace in the storm because I was too busy trying to convince Him to get me out of there—post haste. Sound familiar?

Wouldn't it be wonderful to experience the "peace that passes all understanding" before the storm so that after the storm we can say without feeling embarrassed, "I knew You would take care of me."

That would be worth its weight in gold.

✧✧✧

"You will keep in perfect peace him whose mind is steadfast, because he trusts in you." ISAIAH 26:3 (NIV)

"Peace I leave with you; my peace I give you. I do not give to you as the world gives. Do not let your hearts be troubled and do not be afraid." JOHN 14:27 (NIV)

"I have told you these things, so that in me you may have peace. In this world you will have trouble. But take heart! I have overcome the world." JOHN 16:33 (NIV)

"Do not be anxious about anything, but in everything, by prayer and petition, with thanksgiving, present your requests to God. And the peace of God, which transcends all understanding, will guard your hearts and your minds in Christ Jesus." PHILIPPIANS 4:6, 7 (NIV)

"Now may the Lord of peace himself give you peace at all times and in every way. The Lord be with all of you." 2 THESSALONIANS 3:16 (NIV)

The Secret of
VICTORY

Be alert. Continue strong in the faith.
Have courage, and be strong.

1 CORINTHIANS 16:13

HE TRIP was every bit as bad as Landon feared it would be. His cousin was a troublemaker. Every time Landon was with him, he got into trouble.

"He has a way of making me do bad things," he'd explained to Josh before the trip. "Like last year, he sneaked into an X-rated movie theater. I didn't want to go, but I knew if I didn't, I'd feel like a geek. So I went."

"Sounds like he's a bad influence on you," Josh replied.

"Sometimes it feels like he's more than a bad influence. It feels like he has control of me."

Josh went into his study and returned with the book of secrets. He removed the key from around his neck and gave it and the book to Landon. "When temptation comes, get off by yourself and read the story entitled, 'The Song of the King.' It will give you strength."

✧ ✧ ✧

The temptation came sooner than Landon expected. Even as their parents were greeting each other in the front yard, his cousin leaned over and whispered, "We're gonna party tonight."

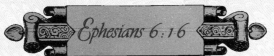
Ephesians 6:16

Later when the two were alone, he told Landon, "After the folks are in bed, we'll sneak out. I know a girl whose folks are out of town. Everybody will be there!"

Landon tried to think of an excuse, but he couldn't. All evening he dreaded the encounter. He didn't know what to do. Then he remembered the book of secrets. He told everyone good night, nodded at his cousin's wink, and went into the guest room.

"Tell me what to do, Lord," he prayed as he sat on the bed and unlocked the book. He found the chapter and started to read.

The Song of the King

*T*he three knights sat at the table and listened as the prince spoke. *"My father, the king, has pledged the hand of my sister to the first of you who can prove himself worthy."*

The prince paused to let the men take in the news. He looked at their faces—each weathered from miles and scarred from battles. The kingdom knew no stronger warriors than these three. And these three soldiers knew of no fairer maiden than the daughter of the king.

Each knight had asked the king for her hand. The king had promised only an opportunity— a test to see which was worthy of his daughter. And now the time for the test had arrived.

"Your test is a journey," the prince explained, "a journey to the king's castle by way of Hemlock."

"The forest?" one knight quickly inquired.

"The forest," answered the prince.

There was silence as the knights pondered the words. Each felt a stab of fear. They knew the danger of Hemlock, a dark and deadly place. Parts of it were so thick with trees that the sunlight never found the floor.

It was the home of the Hopenots—small, sly creatures with yellow eyes. Hopenots were not strong, but they were clever, and they were many. Some people believed the Hopenots were lost travelers changed by the darkness. But no one really knew for sure.

"Will we travel alone?" Carlisle spoke—a strange question to come from the strongest of the three knights. His fierce sword was known throughout the kingdom. But even this steely soldier knew better than to travel Hemlock unaccompanied.

"You may each select one companion."

"But the forest is dark. The trees make the sky black. How will we find the castle?" This time it was Alon who spoke. He was not as strong as Carlisle, but much quicker. He was famous for his speed. Alon left trails of baffled enemies whose grasp he'd escaped by ducking into trees or scampering

over walls. But swiftness is worthless if you have no direction. So Alon asked, "How can we find the way?"

The prince nodded, reached into his sack, and pulled out an ivory flute. "There are only two of these," he explained. "This one and another in the possession of the king."

He put the instrument to his lips and played a soft, sweet aria. Never had the knights heard such soothing music. "My father's flute plays the same song. His song will guide you to the castle."

"How is that?" Alon asked.

"Three times a day the king will play from the castle wall. When the sun rises, when the sun peaks, and when the sun sets. Listen for him. Follow his song and you will find the castle."

"There is only one other flute like this one?"

"Only one."

"And you and your father play the same music?"

"Yes."

It was Cassidon inquiring. Cassidon was known for his alertness. He saw what others missed. He knew the home of a traveler by the dirt on his boot. He knew the truth of a story by the eyes of the teller. He could tell the size of a marching army by the number of scattered birds in flight.

Carlisle and Alon wondered why he asked about the flute. It wouldn't be very long before they found out.

"Consider the danger and choose your companion carefully," the prince cautioned. And so they did. The next morning the three knights mounted their horses and entered Hemlock. Behind each rode the chosen companion.

✧✧✧

The knock at the door startled Landon. He looked up from the book to see his cousin in the doorway. "Everybody is going to bed," he whispered. "I'll be back in a few minutes."

And then loud enough for everyone to hear he said, "'Night, Landon. See you in the morning."

Landon groaned. "These knights aren't the only travelers in a dangerous forest," he muttered to himself as he turned his attention back to the book.

✧✧✧

For the people in the king's castle, the days of waiting passed slowly. All knew of the test. And all wondered which knight would win the princess. Three times a day the king sent the music soaring into the trees of Hemlock. And three times a day the people stopped their work to listen.

After many days and countless songs, a watchman spotted two figures stumbling out of the forest into the clearing. No one could tell who they were. They were too far from the castle. The men had no horses, weapons, or armor.

"Hurry," commanded the king to his guards, "bring them in. Give them medical treatment and food, but don't tell anyone who they are. Dress the knight as a prince, and we will see their faces tonight at the banquet."

He then dismissed the crowds and told them to prepare for the feast.

That evening a festive spirit filled the banquet hall. At every table the people tried to guess which knight had survived Hemlock Forest.

Finally, the moment came to present the victor. At the king's signal the people became quiet, and he began to play the flute. Once again the ivory instrument sang. The people turned to see who would enter.

Many thought it would be Carlisle, the strongest. Others felt it would be Alon, the swiftest. But it was neither. The knight who survived the journey was Cassidon, the wisest.

He strode quickly across the floor, following the sound of the flute one final time and bowing before the king.

"Tell us of your journey," he was instructed. The people leaned forward to listen.

"The Hopenots were treacherous," Cassidon began. "They attacked, but we resisted. They took our horses, but we continued. What nearly destroyed us, though, was something far worse."

"What was that?" asked the princess.

"They imitated."

"They imitated?" asked the king.

"Yes, my king. They imitated. Each time the song of your flute would enter the forest, a hundred flutes would begin to play. All around us we heard music—songs from every direction."

"I do not know what became of Carlisle and Alon," he continued, "but I know strength and speed will not help one hear the right flute."

The king asked the question that was on everyone's lips. "Then how did you hear my song?"

"I chose the right companion," he answered as he motioned for his fellow traveler to enter. The people gasped. It was the prince. In his hand he carried the flute.

"I knew there was only one who could play the song as you do," Cassidon explained. "So I asked him to travel with me. As we journeyed, he played. I learned your song so well that though a thousand false flutes tried to hide your music, I could still hear you. I knew your song and followed it."

❖ ❖ ❖

As Landon closed the book, a note fell out. He picked it up.

"Follow the song of the King, Landon. Love, Josh."

"Yeah, Josh. That's what I will do." Landon resolved aloud. "That's what I will do."

Minutes later his cousin's face peeked through the crack of the door. "Come on, Landon. Let's get out of here."

"I've decided not to go."

"What? Come on, don't be a nerd. Let's go have some fun."

"No thanks." Landon's voice was steady. "I'm staying home."

And then with a smile he added, "I've got some music to listen to."

Victory

The Christian life can be likened to walking up an incline. Jesus called it "the narrow road." Along the way are many opportunities (temptations) to stop, or at least to become distracted. Our potent enemy (Satan) has littered our path with every stupid, pleasurable, and deadly thing at his disposal. Too often we fall for the "apple" he offers. We think it's just "kids' stuff" or exploring what's out there. But Eve found out that it's much better to avoid getting ensnared than to try to get out of the trap. Many of us, as adults, have learned this same hard lesson.

But there's a secret here that might help. It's called discernment. If we could quickly recognize sin for what it is and not be fooled by the packaging, we could resist it every time. If you knew that the beautiful candy-coated apple was really poison, you wouldn't think of biting into it.

I have discovered an encouraging truth—the lure of something gets weaker the longer I resist it. Sure, at first it seems almost overwhelming, as if there is no way to refuse it, but that perception is only an illusion. Temptation is going to come to you through an enticing picture in a magazine or through a "friend." It will not look like poison, but it is. Everything inside you will scream, "Go ahead and take a small bite." Don't. The secret to staying on the road is making the decision to resist long before the offer comes.

"Be self-controlled and alert. Your enemy the devil prowls around like a roaring lion looking for someone to devour. Resist him, standing firm in the faith, because you know that your brothers throughout the world are undergoing the same kind of sufferings." 1 PETER 5:8, 9 (NIV)

"Submit yourselves, then, to God. Resist the devil, and he will flee from you." JAMES 4:7 (NIV)

"Put on the full armor of God so that you can take your stand against the devil's schemes. For our struggle is not against flesh and blood, but against the rulers, against the authorities, against the powers of this dark world and against the spiritual forces of evil in the heavenly realms. Therefore put on the full armor of God, so that when the day of evil comes, you may be able to stand your ground." EPHESIANS 6:11–13 (NIV)

The Secret of
GROWTH

But God knows the way I take, and when he
has tested me, I will come out as gold.

JOB 23:10

ERIC LOOKED up at Landon and Shannon as they entered the restaurant. "Do you know what this is all about?" he asked.

"Not a clue," responded Landon as he sat down. "There was a message from Josh on our answering machine last night telling us he would meet us here at 9:00 A.M. So here we are."

"Maybe he just wants to buy us breakfast," Shannon volunteered, eyeing the selections behind the counter.

"Don't think so. He told me to be ready to get dirty," Eric said.

Landon produced a pair of work gloves. "Josh even told me to bring these."

"This is weird," observed Shannon. "A Saturday morning meeting with no reason?"

"Sure there's a reason." The voice was Josh's. They hadn't seen him come in. He pulled out a chair and sat down, placing a burlap bag on the table.

"What's the big mystery, Josh?" Eric asked.

"Yeah," Landon continued, "why did you want to see us and why did you want us in work clothes?"

The Chisel

"Well, I have several reasons," Josh began. "The first one is Amanda, the second is the Pirates, and the third is the school play."

All three kids looked at Josh, partly surprised and partly embarrassed. The first to speak was Landon.

"Who told you about Amanda?"

"Your dad."

"What did he say?"

"He said she dumped you for the basketball player."

Landon looked down at the table. "Raw deal. The guy is a jerk."

"Well," Josh comforted, "you're not the only guy who got the shaft this week." And he looked straight at Eric.

"The Pirates game?" Eric asked.

"Didn't your big brother ask you to go?"

"Yeah, but then he changed his mind. Said he'd rather take a date."

"Probably taking Amanda," Shannon chuckled.

Josh spoke quickly before either of the boys could respond. "Your week hasn't been that great either, has it, Shannon?"

"Melva told you?"

"Yep."

"I didn't get the lead in the play, Josh. I practiced for two months, and ended up with only a small part—just a few lines."

Landon was beginning to understand the purpose of the meeting. "You've got something brewing, don't you, Josh? You knew each of us had a bad week and you . . ."

"I brought you something."

"A gift to make me feel better?" piped Shannon.

"No, a gift to help you understand better," explained Josh. He reached into the burlap bag and handed each one a different object.

"For you, Landon, a lump of clay. Eric, I brought you an old pocket knife. And Shannon, a new steel horse's bit."

The three stared at the strange objects.

Landon spoke first. "Uhhh . . . thanks, Josh. Just what I wanted—a lump of clay."

Eric knew something was up. "Come on, Josh. What's this about?"

"Here's a clue," Josh said, laying the book of secrets on the table and removing the key from around his neck. He opened it and handed it to Eric. "Read the riddle on that page for us."

You're glad I came when I'm gone, but you wish I'd leave when I'm there.
It hurts when I help. I stretch when I strengthen.
Who am I?

Eric, Shannon, and Landon looked at each other, puzzled.

Josh grinned. "It's all right. I've got an assignment for each of you that should help you discover the answer. On each of these sheets of paper is an address. Go to it and tell the person that I sent you. There you'll be instructed what to do. I'll meet you back here in four hours."

The three looked at each other and smiled. "Sounds fun!" Shannon said.

"Well, okay," Eric said slowly. "But I sure can't figure out what a pocket knife can teach me about missing a baseball game."

"Or what this piece of clay can teach me about girls," Landon agreed.

"Just trust me," Josh smiled.

Shannon didn't have far to go to find the address on her slip of paper. It was the horse stables at the park district on the edge of town.

"My name is Shannon," she told the woman at the front gate.

"Oh, you're the girl Josh told me to look for. Did you bring the bit?"

Shannon held it up so the lady could see.

"Great. Take the dirt road to the pasture just beyond the barn and wait there."

As Shannon turned toward the path the lady added, "Learn a lot."

The trainer was already at the pasture when Shannon arrived. "Hi, I'm Bill . . . and this is Thunder," he said, pointing to a charcoal gray colt pacing back and forth across the grassy lot.

"Well, are you ready to get started?" he asked.

Shannon looked at Bill, and then at the colt, and back at Bill, who was climbing over the wooden rail fence.

"Sure!" she said. "By the way, what are we doing?"

"You'll see," Bill said. "Just follow me and don't move too fast when we get close to Thunder."

About the time Shannon stroked Thunder's mane for the first time, Eric was sitting on his bike at a street corner reading the paper Josh had given him. "Go to the intersection of Hoppers and Bluefield," it read. And that's where he was. *What do I do now?* he thought to himself.

But before he had time to answer, someone tapped him on the shoulder. "Are you Eric?"

He turned and looked. It was a policeman. "Uh, yessir."

"Did you bring your pocket knife?"

"Yessir."

"Then follow me."

"Do you know Josh?"

"I know Josh," the man replied, turned and began walking away. When he saw that Eric hadn't moved, he stopped again.

"Come on, we'll be late."

Eric walked his bike several feet behind the officer. The policeman didn't explain where they were going and Eric didn't ask.

After a few minutes they came upon a large building. The policeman entered, but Eric stopped. The officer turned and spoke again. "It's okay. Come on in."

Above the door were the words, "Bluefield Police Station."

Landon's address took him to a house not far from his own. In fact, when he took the shortcut to school, he pedaled right past it. It was a simple house with tall trees and a big yard. A sign hung on the fence: "Art classes daily." Even from the street he could see the large shed in the back. He'd often wondered what was in there.

"Guess I'll find out today," he said to himself as he laid his bike in the grass and walked up to the door.

A woman wearing a full-length apron answered his knock. She was young. About the age of his English teacher, who had just graduated from college. "Yes?" she asked.

He looked down at the paper. "Ask for Pamela," it read. So he did. "I'm looking for Pamela."

"That's me; you must be Landon. You're taller than I'd imagined."

Landon straightened his shoulders. "Come with me," she said. "Josh has told me all about you. Let me see what you brought."

He handed her the clay and she inspected it. "Just right for making a bowl," she observed as the two walked into the shed.

Around the room sat half-a-dozen people, back to back, on small stools, each busy working.

"I saved you the wheel in the corner," Pamela explained, leading Landon over to a workbench beneath the window. "But before we go there, let's get the clay ready."

"Uh, what are we doing?"

"Josh told me to teach you something about pottery." And with a twinkle in her eye she added, "Girl problems? Let's begin by kneading?"

"Kneeling?"

"No, *kneading*. It's the process of preparing the clay for the wheel. Here, take this and put it on the bench," she instructed, handing Landon the lump of clay.

Landon, still confused, did what she said.

"Now press it with the strong muscles at the base of your palm. Stretch it out and then fold it over and do it again. Press it hard, as hard as you can. The harder you push, the firmer it will be. I'll be back in a few minutes."

On the windowsill Landon saw a variety of bowls, plates, and vases. "Is that what I'm going to make?"

"We'll try."

Soon Landon forgot the mystery of his trip and was caught up in the wonder of pottery.

Later that afternoon, back at the restaurant, Landon gave his report first. He was especially fascinated with the wheel, and it was the wheel that dominated his report to Josh, Eric, and Shannon.

"It's a flat disc that goes around and around," he explained, moving his hands in circles. "Pamela told me the most important step is getting the clay centered on the wheel. If it's off-center, the clay will fly off. But if it's centered just right, you can shape it into whatever form you want!"

"It took me a while to get the feel of it, but with time I could cup my hands around the wet clay and it would respond to my hand. If I squeezed it, the clay got taller. If I loosened my hand it got fatter. Pam showed me how to make a hole and shape a collar and, well, look!"

Landon proudly produced a small bowl. "We'll paint it next week!" he announced.

"Can I show them what I did?"

"Sure, Shannon," Josh nodded.

Shannon reached into her pocket and pulled out a Polaroid photo of her standing with a bridled Thunder.

"You rode a horse?" Eric asked.

"No, I helped the trainer get this colt used to wearing a bridle. It's never worn a saddle or anything, so we spent the morning introducing him to a halter, which goes over his head like a bridle but doesn't have the steel bit in the horse's mouth."

"What did he do at first when you tried to put it on?" Josh asked.

"Well, he tried to run away, but Bill held on to him."

"And then?"

"Thunder kept ducking his head, but I eventually slipped it on over his ears, and we let him run until he was used to the halter."

"He really didn't like it, though, when we replaced the halter with a bridle! It took us fifteen minutes to get the thing on. But we just left the bridle on until he didn't seem bothered by it anymore. After that we took it off and sent him to the barn for his lunch."

"Why did you have to do all that?" Eric asked.

"Bill said that without putting Thunder through this, he'd never be tame enough to be ridden. And without that bit in his mouth, he wouldn't obey the riders' directions to turn or stop."

"Tell us where you went, Eric," Josh asked.

"Well, at first I was scared. A policeman took me to the basement at the police station where four guys were sitting on a bench with knives."

"Were they crooks?" Shannon asked.

"No, they were cops. They were carving pieces of wood. They meet every Saturday before they go to work. It's their hobby."

"What did you make?" Josh spoke up.

"Well, I'm not finished yet," Eric replied, reaching into a sack. "It's going to be . . ."

". . . A duck!" Shannon interrupted.

"Yeah," Eric beamed, "I'm making a duck. First we drew the pattern on wood with chalk. Then we chiseled away the big pieces. Then they showed me how to carve the details. They told me that sanding the wood is really important. It makes the wood smooth."

"Gets rid of the rough spots," Josh added. "Kind of like bridling a horse so that riders can enjoy a comfortable ride, right, Shannon?"

"Yeah."

"Kind of like kneading the clay so that it comes out smooth, right, Landon?"

"Yeah, Josh," Landon answered, again suspecting that something was coming. He was right.

Josh leaned forward, reopened the book of secrets, and said, "Here is what I want you guys to learn." Then he motioned to Shannon to read.

"Consider it pure joy, my brothers, whenever you face trials of many kinds, because you know that the testing of your faith develops perseverance. Perseverance must finish its work so that you may be mature and complete, not lacking anything." (James 1:2–4 NIV)

Josh leaned forward, picking up Landon's bowl. "Here is what I want you guys to learn," he said. "This morning I gave you some useless objects—a piece of wood, a lump of clay, and a steel bit. You took them and put them into the skillful hands of a carver, a potter, and a trainer. After some time in the hands of the right person, what was a useless object became useful."

Shannon looked confused. "I don't get it. You mean if Landon shapes clay, then girls won't ditch him?"

"No," Josh said, smiling, "what I mean is that Landon *is* the clay. Eric *is* the wood. You *are* the young horse. We are all being shaped by the Master."

"Oh." Eric smiled. "I get it. We are being shaped in God's hands."

"That is absolutely true. We are each in God's hands, and He is guiding us like you guided the horse, Shannon. He is molding us like you molded this bowl, Landon. God is trimming us just as you shaved the wood to make a duck."

"Ohhh," Landon and Eric replied at the same time.

"I don't get it," Shannon spoke. "Not getting the lead in the play is God's way of helping me?"

"Shannon," Josh replied, "God can use anything to help you grow."

"Growth!" Landon blurted. The other three turned and stared.

"What?" Eric asked.

"Growth." Landon smiled. "That's the answer to the riddle. Growth hurts when it helps. Growth stretches when it strengthens."

"Yeah." Eric caught on. "And when growth happens, you don't like it. But after it's over, you are glad it came."

"Good job!" Josh smiled. "Looks like you learned the secret of growth. Want to read it?"

Shannon spoke first. "I do."

Josh handed her the book of secrets and showed her the secret to read.

What is painful today has a purpose tomorrow.

Josh looked at the three and said, "Next time things don't work out with a girl or a game or anything else, remember you're in God's hands. He's making you into something special. And He doesn't make mistakes."

Growth

G*rowth.* You can feel the pain in that word right off the bat. How many times have our children complained of "growing pains"? Well, spiritually the same thing happens. Growth comes mostly through pain. We often give our children the impression that difficulties are to be avoided at all cost and that hard circumstances reflect the *absence* of God in our lives. But just as a sculptor uses a chisel to chip away the rough exterior to get at the beauty underneath, so God continually shapes us into the image of His Son. He wants us to be works of art in the shape of Christ. Every challenge, every valley, and every moment of pain is the vehicle to get there.

Here is a secret. When you ask for patience, God will usually allow circumstances to help you develop it. The same with courage, peace, trust, and most other godly attributes. You can make that process short or long, depending on whether you choose to submit or to fight it every step of the way. Oh, I forgot to mention that the process ends up with us refined as gold. I like that part.

"And we pray this in order that you may live a life worthy of the Lord and may please him in every way: bearing fruit in every good work, growing in the knowledge of God, being strengthened with all power according to his glorious might so that you may have great endurance and patience, and joyfully giving thanks to the Father, who has qualified you to share in the inheritance of the saints in the kingdom of light." COLOSSIANS 1:10–12 (NIV)

". . . I will refine them like silver and test them like gold." ZECHARIAH 13:9 (NIV)

The Secret of
LOVE

A wife of noble character who can find?
She is worth far more than rubies.

PROVERBS 31:10 (NIV)

MUST WARN YOU, reader, before you begin. These words are ancient jewels mined from the quarry of my life. Read them only if you dare treasure them. For it would be better to never know, than to know and not obey.
The hand which writes them is now old, wrinkled from the sun and labor. But the mind which guides them is wise—

wise from years
wise from failures
wise from heartache.
I am Asmara, merchant of fine stones.

"He had a leathery face," Josh had explained to Eric, "and a snowy white beard. The lines around his eyes were deep as canyons. He wore a black hat with a short bill and carried an ebony cane topped with a raven's head.

"We became friends in the port city of Morocco, meeting at the same cafe every morning for a summer. At first by chance, but with time by plan, we met and talked. He

The Blessing

was nearly ninety years of age—an old traveler near the end of his life. I was barely twenty, a young missionary on my maiden voyage."

"What did he teach you?" Eric had asked.

"He taught me about the one jewel he never held."

"What was that?"

"Read and see. I was so moved by his story that I gave him my journal and asked him to write it. The words you read are his. But the lesson he teaches is yours. If you are willing."

Eric was more than willing. He needed some guidance. That morning at baseball practice he had come upon his friends huddled in the dugout. "What's up?" he asked peering over their shoulders.

No one responded; they just snickered and invited him to sit down. On the floor was a box of magazines—magazines full of pictures of naked women. "Go ahead, Eric. Pick one up," one of the boys urged. "I found them in my brother's closet."

"Yeah, Eric, go ahead. It's okay," spoke another.

"Come on, Eric, no one will know."

"Maybe later," was all he could think to say, and he hurried out onto the baseball field.

Later he told Josh that he was confused. "Maybe the guys were right. After all, it's only pictures."

But Josh wasn't confused. He spoke as if he knew exactly what Eric was facing. "Be careful, Eric. Lust dresses well to please the buyer."

"What?"

"What you experienced this morning could destroy you."

"It was just a magazine."

Josh responded firmly. "It wasn't just a magazine, Eric. It was a *bad* magazine. A magazine that teaches a lie."

"A lie?" Eric was surprised at Josh's firmness.

"That's right, a lie. A lie about love and beauty. Listen to me, Eric. Love is much more than a pretty face or body. Love is from the inside, not the outside."

When Josh finished speaking, he gave Eric the key and the book and sent him to the park to read the story. Eric found an empty bench, sat down, and opened the book. The handwriting was broad.

✧✧✧

I am a seller of stones. I travel from city to city. I buy jewels from the diggers in one land and sell them to the buyers in another. I have weathered nights on stormy waters. I have walked days through desert heat. I have dined with kings. I have drunk with paupers. My hands have held the finest rubies and stroked the deepest furs. But I would trade it all for the one jewel I never knew.

It was not for lack of opportunity that I never held it. There was a chance in Madrid when I was young. No, it was not for lack of opportunity. It was for lack of wisdom. The jewel was in my hand, but I exchanged it for an imitation. And now I fear my days will end without my ever knowing the beauty of the precious stone.

✧✧✧

"What stone is he talking about?" Eric said to himself as he turned the page. The answer came in the next line. The ink was bolder and the words underlined.

✧✧✧

I have never known true love.

I have known embraces. I have seen beauty. But I have never known love.

If only I'd learned to recognize love as I have learned to recognize stones.

My father taught me about stones. He was a jewel cutter. He would seat me at a table before a dozen emeralds. "One is true," he would tell me. "The others are false. Find the true jewel."

I would ponder—studying one after the other. Finally I would choose. I was always wrong.

"The secret," he would say, "is not on the surface of the stone; it is inside the stone. A true jewel has a glow. Deep within the gem there is a flame. The surface can always be polished to shine, but with time the sparkle fades. However, the stone that shines from within will never fade."

With the years, my eyes learned to spot true stones. I am never fooled. The stones I purchase are authentic. The gems I sell are true. I have learned to see the light within.

If only I'd learned the same about love.

But I've been foolish, dear reader, and I've been fooled.

I've spent my life in places I shouldn't have been, looking only for someone with sparkling eyes, beautiful hair, a dazzling smile, and fancy clothes. I've searched for a woman with outer beauty, but no true value. And now I am left with emptiness.

Once I almost found her. Many years ago in Madrid, I met the daughter of a farmer. Her ways were simple. Her love was pure. Her eyes were honest. But her looks were plain. She would have loved me. She would have held me through every season. Within her was a glow of devotion the like of which I've never seen since.

But I continued looking for someone whose beauty would outshine the rest.

How many times since have I longed for that farm girl's kind heart, her sweet smile, her

45

faithfulness? If only I'd known that true beauty is found inside, not outside. If only I'd known, how many tears would I have saved?

I'd trade in a moment a thousand rare gems for the true heart of one who would have loved me.

Dear reader, heed my warning. Look closely at the stones before you open your purse. True love glows from within and grows stronger with the passage of time.

Heed my caution. Look for the purest gem. Look deep within the heart to find the greatest beauty of all. And when you find that gem, hold onto her and never let her go.

For in her you have been granted a treasure worth far more than rubies.

Eric looked at the last words for a few minutes before he closed the book. He hadn't noticed that on the bench across from him were Josh and Melva. He only looked up when Josh began to speak.

"When Asmara returned my journal, he said these words, 'Choose true love when you are young so you won't be lonely when you are old.' Then he turned and left. That was the last time I ever saw him, Eric. I'll never forget how sad he looked." And taking Melva's hand he added, "And I'll never regret the choice I made."

Josh leaned forward and looked squarely into the eyes of his young friend, "Turn the page and read the secret of love."

Eric did, and this is what he saw:

Seek beauty and miss love.

But seek love and find both.

Love

W hat's love got to do with it?" asked a popular rock song. Unfortunately, this is the philosophy of our culture. A preoccupation with sex seems so ingrained in every movie, magazine, and television show that it's no wonder that the family is in jeopardy.

The glue that God designed to hold it all together is *love* in *marriage.* Not sex. Sex outside of God's perfect plan is empty. The lure of illicit sex is an illusion, however powerful it seems. And Satan achieves a gigantic victory when a person is willing to pursue this illusion. Marriage is where sex belongs. And that's the *only* place where it's fulfilling because God intended it that way.

Since time has a way of changing our appearance over the years, it's a comfort to me that my mate is going to love me when there won't be a whole lot to look at. But then again, that's why I married her, and I intend to love her when she is no longer attractive as well.

"Love is patient, love is kind. It does not envy, it does not boast, it is not proud. It is not rude, it is not self-seeking, it is not easily angered, it keeps no record of wrongs. Love does not delight in evil but rejoices with the truth. It always protects, always trusts, always hopes, always perseveres." 1 CORINTHIANS 13:4 (NIV)

"Your beauty should not come from outward adornment, such as braided hair and the wearing of gold jewelry and fine clothes. Instead, it should be that of your inner self, the unfading beauty of a gentle and quiet spirit, which is of great worth in God's sight." 1 PETER 3:3 (NIV)

"Do not love the world or anything in the world. If anyone loves the world, the love of the Father is not in him. For everything in the world—the cravings of sinful man, the lust of his eyes and the boasting of what he has and does—comes not from the Father but from the world. The world and its desires pass away, but the man who does the will of God lives forever." 1 JOHN 2:15 (NIV)

The Secret of
GREATNESS

. . . We are not trying to please people, but God . . .

—I Thessalonians 2:4

. . . Whoever wants to be great among you
must be your servant . . .

—Matthew 20:26

HANNON'S DAY had been full of surprises. The first one came as she was leaving Josh's house.

"Carry this with you," he'd said, handing her the book of secrets and the key. "Take it home?"

"You may need it." And that's all he'd said.

So as Shannon walked, she kicked the leaves and wondered what Josh knew that she didn't. He'd never entrusted her with his book before. He didn't even let her take it to share with her class at school. But now he wanted her to take it home?

As she turned the corner toward her house, she saw the second surprise of the day. Her father's car was in the driveway.

"Wonder why he's home so early," she asked herself.

She smiled. "He's up to something." Shannon loved her father because he was so much fun. In the mornings they'd put the bread crumbs out for the birds. At night he always had a story or a song. No matter how many times he'd fake bumping his nose on

The Servant

the wall, she still giggled. Some days he'd surprise her by showing up at the school cafeteria. One time he'd tacked on the wall a list of all the people who loved her.

She didn't know why he was home, but she was excited to see him. As she entered she saw him in the study. "Dad?" He didn't look up. He was slouched in his office chair with his face in his hand, shaking his head.

"Dad," she asked as she walked near, "are you sick?"

He still didn't respond.

"What's wrong, Daddy?"

He looked up with surprise. "Oh, Shannon, I didn't hear you come in."

His eyes were red, his cheeks moist.

"What's wrong, Dad?"

"Oh, it's nothing, honey."

"Tell me what happened."

"Just some problems at work. Don't worry about it."

"Daddy . . ." Shannon stretched the word, using that come-on-let's-talk tone of voice.

He sighed and lifted her onto his lap.

"Oh, it's the guys at work, Shannon. I really thought I was going to get a promotion."

"A what?"

"I thought I was going to get a better job. But the boss chose someone else instead of me."

"Why?"

"He says I'm not good enough, that I didn't have enough drive to get ahead."

"What does it matter what he thinks, Dad?"

"Well, it hurts when people say things like that. Remember when Jennifer didn't ask you to the slumber party?"

"Yeah, I was the only one not invited."

"How did it make you feel?"

Shannon thought for a moment and then answered, "Left out."

"That's how I feel. I've lost something that seemed important to me."

For a few moments neither of them spoke. Shannon just sat on his lap, looking out the window. She'd never seen her dad this sad. In fact, she didn't know grown-ups got this discouraged. Suddenly she understood why Josh had loaned her the book.

She got down and took it out of her pack. "I want to read you a story, Dad."

"You want to read me a story?"

"Yeah, it's one Josh showed me." She climbed back into his lap and began to read.

The Wemmicks

The Wemmicks were small wooden people. Each of the wooden people was carved by a woodworker named Eli. His workshop sat on a hill overlooking their village.

Every Wemmick was different. Some had big noses, others had large eyes. Some were tall and others were short. Some wore hats, others wore coats. But all were made by the same carver and all lived in the village.

And all day, every day, the Wemmicks did the same thing: They gave each other stickers. Each Wemmick had a box of golden star stickers and a box of gray dot stickers. Up and down the streets all over the city, people could be seen sticking stars or dots on one another.

The pretty ones, those with smooth wood and fine paint, always got stars. But if the wood was rough or the paint chipped, the Wemmicks gave dots.

The talented ones got stars, too. Some could lift big sticks high above their heads or jump over tall boxes. Still others knew big words or could sing very pretty songs. Everyone gave them stars.

Some Wemmicks had stars all over them! Every time they got a star it made them feel so good that they did something else and got another star.

Others, though, could do little. They got dots.

Punchinello was one of these. He tried to jump high like the others, but he always fell. And when he fell, the others would gather around and give him dots.

Sometimes when he fell, it would scar his wood, so the people would give him more dots.

He would try to explain why he fell and say something silly, and the Wemmicks would give him more dots.

After a while he had so many dots that he didn't want to go outside. He was afraid he would do something dumb such as forget his hat or step in the water, and then people would give him another dot. In fact, he had so many gray dots that some people would come up and give him one without a reason.

"He deserves lots of dots," the wooden people would agree with one another. "He's not a good wooden person."

After a while Punchinello believed them. "I'm not a good Wemmick," he would say.

The few times he went outside, he hung around other Wemmicks who had a lot of dots. He felt better around them.

One day he met a Wemmick who was unlike any he'd ever met. She had no dots or stars. She was just wooden. Her name was Lucia.

It wasn't that people didn't try to give her stickers; it's just that the stickers didn't stick.

Some admired Lucia for having no dots, so they would run up and give her a star. But it would fall off. Some would look down on her for having no stars, so they would give her a dot. But it wouldn't stay either.

That's the way I want to be, *thought Punchinello.* I don't want anyone's marks. *So he asked the stickerless Wemmick how she did it.*

"It's easy," Lucia replied. "Every day I go see Eli."

"Eli?"

"Yes, Eli. The woodcarver. I sit in the workshop with him."

"Why?"

"Why don't you find out for yourself? Go up the hill. He's there." And with that the Wemmick with no marks turned and skipped away.

"But he won't want to see me!" Punchinello cried out. Lucia didn't hear. So Punchinello went home. He sat near a window and watched the wooden people as they scurried around giving each other stars and dots. "It's not right," he muttered to himself. And he resolved to go see Eli.

He walked up the narrow path to the top of the hill and stepped into the big shop. His wooden eyes widened at the size of everything. The stool was as tall as he was. He had to stretch on his tiptoes to see the top of the workbench. A hammer was as long as his arm. Punchinello swallowed hard. "I'm not staying here!" and he turned to leave.

Then he heard his name.

"Punchinello?" The voice was deep and strong.

Punchinello stopped.

"Punchinello! How good to see you. Come and let me have a look at you."

Punchinello turned slowly and looked at the large bearded craftsman. "You know my name?" the little Wemmick asked.

"Of course I do. I made you."

Eli stooped down and picked him up and set him on the bench. "Hmm," the maker spoke thoughtfully as he inspected the gray circles. "Looks like you've been given some bad marks."

"I didn't mean to, Eli. I really tried hard."

"Oh, you don't have to defend yourself to me, child. I don't care what the other Wemmicks think."

"You don't?"

"No, and you shouldn't either. Who are they to give stars or dots? They're Wemmicks just like you. What they think doesn't matter, Punchinello. All that matters is what I think. And I think you are pretty special."

Punchinello laughed. "Me, special? Why? I can't walk fast. I can't jump. My paint is peeling. Why do I matter to you?"

Eli looked at Punchinello, put his hands on those small wooden shoulders, and spoke very slowly. "Because you're mine. That's why you matter to me."

Punchinello had never had anyone look at him like this—much less his maker. He didn't know what to say.

"Every day I've been hoping you'd come," Eli explained.

"I came because I met someone who had no marks."

"I know. She told me about you."

"Why don't the stickers stay on her?"

"Because she has decided that what I think is more important than what they think. The stickers only stick if you let them."

"What?"

"The stickers only stick if they matter to you. The more you trust my love, the less you care about their stickers."

"I'm not sure I understand."

"You will, but it will take time. You've got a lot of marks. For now, just come to see me every day and let me remind you how much I care."

Eli lifted Punchinello off the bench and set him on the ground.

"Remember," Eli said as the Wemmick walked out the door. "You are special because I made you. And I don't make mistakes."

Punchinello didn't stop, but in his heart he thought, "I think he really means it."

And when he did, a dot fell to the ground.

Shannon looked up at her dad. He was smiling. "How did you know I needed to hear that?" he asked.

"I didn't. God did."

"Well, I feel like Punchinello."

"When he was covered with dots?" she asked.

"No, when the first one fell off."

Greatness

Greatness. The very word sounds good. There isn't a parent who doesn't want greatness for his or her child. Where most of us part company is over the way to achieve greatness. If you asked any modern child to name a great person, he would probably name a famous athlete, movie star, or rock musician—at least someone in the public eye. Let's face it, that is what most of us think of as greatness. Yet we who are called by Christ's name ought to use His definition of greatness. He said a person who chooses to *serve* is great. Yes, you heard it correctly—*serve.* Do we encourage our children to become servants? We should, since Jesus said servanthood is the path to greatness. Then let's watch the blessing of God pour out on their lives.

"Not so with you. Instead, whoever wants to become great among you must be your servant, and whoever wants to be first must be your slave—just as the Son of Man did not come to be served, but to serve, and to give his life as a ransom for many." MATTHEW 20:26 (NIV)

"If anyone wants to be first, he must be the very last, and the servant of all." MARK 9:35 (NIV)

"Humility and the fear of the Lord bring wealth and honor and life." PROVERBS 22:4 (NIV)

The Secret of
LIFE

Rejoice and be glad, because you have a great
reward waiting for you in heaven.

MATTHEW 5:12

ANDON SWALLOWED HARD and folded the note. His teacher watched as he put it in his pocket.

"Is something wrong?" she asked.

"May I be excused?" he asked her. "My sister is waiting for me in the hall."

"Sure."

Shannon's face was tear-streaked. Behind her stood Eric, his hands on her shoulders, his face solemn.

"How did you find out?" Landon asked them.

"Melva called my mom," Eric replied. "Mom called the school office. Josh is in Medical Center hospital. They took him there this morning."

"Something happened to his heart, Landon." Shannon began to cry. "Something is wrong with his heart."

✧✧✧

Melva was the only person in the waiting room. When she saw Eric, Landon, and Shannon, she smiled.

"Josh will be glad to see you," she told them.

Welcome Home

"Will they let us in?" Landon asked.

"For a few minutes."

Shannon sat next to Melva. "Is he going to be okay?"

Melva spoke softly. "Josh is very sick. His heart is weak. The doctors just don't know." Her voice was firm as she spoke, but her eyes filled with tears.

"You can come in now." It was the nurse at the door. They followed her into the intensive care ward.

A circle of ten rooms surrounded the nurses' station. Behind each glass wall was a patient. Some were bandaged. Others were in traction. Others, like Josh, had tubes inserted in their arms and wires taped to their skin.

They'd never seen Josh so still. He lay on his back, eyes closed. Above his head a monitor was beeping with each heartbeat. A plastic mask connected to an oxygen hose covered his nose and mouth.

"It helps him breathe," Melva explained.

Landon and Eric stopped at the foot of the bed, but Shannon went up to Josh's side. She put her little hand in his big one and squeezed. "Can he talk?" she asked.

"Not with the oxygen tube," Melva replied, "but he can hear you." He opened his eyes.

"Look who is here to see you." Melva tried to sound cheerful.

Josh lifted his eyebrows. Eric and Landon walked around the bed and stood at the side of their old friend. They'd never seen him look so tired, so weak. He opened his hand, and both Eric and Landon held it. They didn't know what to say. So no one said anything. Josh's eyes went from face to face.

After a few moments Josh lifted his hand and began to draw in the air. "That means he wants to write something," Melva interpreted. "He has something to tell us."

With a pad on his stomach, Josh scrawled three words and handed them to his wife. She read them, nodded softly, and assured Josh, "I'll take them there and read it."

Just then the nurse entered the room. "I'm sorry," she instructed, "but visiting time is over. You can return at four o'clock."

Josh looked again at each of the children. He forced a smile from beneath the mask. They told him good-bye. Melva leaned over and kissed his forehead. "We'll be back," she whispered and left the room.

He closed his eyes.

As they walked down the hall, Landon asked Melva, "What did he write?"

She handed him the pad. The handwriting was difficult to read. "Obs . . . sto . . . obster. No it's obstet . . ."

"Obstetrical," Melva said. "He wrote 'obstetrical ward'."

"What kind of award is that?" Shannon asked.

"It's not an *award*. It a *ward*. A part of the hospital. Josh wants me to take you there and tell you something."

"What was the third word?" Eric spoke up.

"*Secret*." Melva smiled. "He wants me to read you a secret from the book."

Landon had no idea what 'obstetrical' meant, but he didn't feel like asking. He wasn't in the mood to talk much. Neither was anyone else. It was a quiet group that rode the elevator to the lower floor.

Only Shannon spoke. "A hospital is a sad place," she commented.

"What you are about to see may change your mind," Melva responded as she put her arm around Shannon's shoulder.

The elevator door opened to a room of bright colors and excited people. Bright balloons were painted on one wall, and a colorful aquarium stood in front of the other. Straight ahead were the backs of a row of people—people all looking through a large window. They were laughing and pointing and lifting up small children so they could see.

"It's the baby section!" Eric exclaimed. "This is where my cousin was born."

"Can we see the babies?" Shannon asked.

"That's why we are here," Melva responded.

All four went to the window. Shannon was just tall enough to peek in and see the newborns.

"They are so little!" she exclaimed.

"How old are they?" Landon asked as he looked at the row of bassinets.

"Some were born this morning," Melva answered. "They are brand new!"

It was easy to be amazed at the little bundles wrapped in blankets. Most were asleep, tiny faces soft and relaxed. But a couple of them were crying loudly. "They must be hungry," Eric laughed.

"They've had quite a journey!" Melva added.

"Man," Landon observed, "this room is just the opposite of the room where Josh is. Here everyone is happy and excited. Up there they are quiet and afraid."

"In a way it is different," Melva agreed, "but in another it is very similar."

"How?" asked Landon.

"Why don't we sit down. I'll let Josh explain it to you."

They went to a couch and took a seat. Melva spoke as she took the book of secrets and the key from her purse. "Josh loves to come here. At least once a week he comes to visit."

"Does he like babies?" Shannon asked.

"That's just part of it. He also likes what God teaches him here."

"What?"

"Sometime ago he came and brought the book. As he sat here, he wrote a letter, a letter to you. A letter he wanted me to read to you if anything ever happened to him. Would you like to hear it?"

"Sure," they said, leaning forward to listen. Melva began to read.

Dear Landon, Eric, and Shannon,

This is a very important letter. Melva is reading it to you because something has happened to me. She has brought you here because I want you to learn one of life's most important secrets—the secret of death.

Very few people understand death. Most are afraid of it. Most try to ignore it. Hardly anyone wants to talk about it. But God wants you to understand it. And He doesn't want you to be scared.

Many think death is when you go to sleep. They are wrong. Death is when you finally wake up. Death is when you see what God has seen all along.

I want you to do something for me. I want you to think about these babies. Imagine what has happened to them. They have just left one place and entered another. Just a few hours ago, each one of them was in a mommy's tummy. They were safe. They were warm. They had all they could eat. All they had to do was sleep.

Suddenly they were pushed into a strange world that they had never seen before.

Imagine you could speak to one of these infants before he was born. What if you told him what was about to happen? What if you said, "In just a few minutes you are going to leave this tummy. Your time in here is about up. Before you know it, you will be in a room full of people and lights and noises and smells . . ."

"I don't want to go," the baby might say. "I like it here. Besides I don't know what a 'people' is."

"Oh, you don't need to worry. It's not bad out there," you'd tell the infant. "I mean you have to go to school and take baths."

"What's a school and a bath? None of that sounds good to me. I like it right here."

"But it's dark in there. It's crowded and cramped. Don't worry. You'll be glad you came out."

"Thanks, but no thanks. I'm happy where I am. I want to just stay right here."

60

Landon chuckled at the thought of the baby not wanting to be born. "The baby doesn't have a choice, Melva. He has to come out."

"Yeah," Eric said smiling, "who would want to stay inside a tummy forever?"

"That's exactly what Josh is explaining," Melva answered. "Listen to what he says next."

You see, kids, there comes a time in life when we, like the baby, have to make a journey. Just like the baby has to leave the tummy and enter this world, there comes a time for us to leave this world and go to Heaven.

And most people don't want to go. We act like the little baby in the tummy. We like it where we are. This world may not be perfect, but at least it's familiar, and we don't want to leave.

✧✧✧

Melva's voice choked as she read the next sentence.

✧✧✧

Eric, Landon, and Shannon, it's time for me to leave. It's my turn to go and be with God in Heaven. I don't want you to be afraid. I'm not. It's my time. I accept that. It's okay to be sad, but don't be angry; don't be scared. God knows what He's doing.

I will miss you, but we won't be separated very long. Someday your time will come to leave. And when it's your time, I want you to know I'll be waiting for you. I'll be there when you get there. I'll be one of those proud people standing at the glass.

And standing beside me will be your Father. Your Heavenly Father. We'll be waiting. Don't forget the secret.

Love,
Josh

Melva had barely finished reading the letter when her name was paged over the speaker system, telling her to return to the intensive care unit. She swallowed hard, looked at the kids and said, "Let's go." When they reached Josh's floor, the kids waited outside as Melva went in.

Though she was gone for only a few minutes, it seemed like hours.

When Melva returned, her face looked pale and sad. She sat on the couch and wept softly. "They said he dozed off and never woke up."

"He's gone away?" Shannon asked.

"No, Shannon. He hasn't gone away. He's gone home. He's finally gone home. It's the day he's always dreamed about."

Melva looked at Landon and Eric. "This was in his hands."

She handed Landon his baseball—the same baseball Eric had hit through the window. On it Josh had scribbled 1 Corinthians 15:51.

"What does that verse say?" Landon asked.

Eric picked up a Bible from the table and looked it up. "I am telling you this strange and wonderful secret: we shall not all die, but we shall all be given new bodies" (TLB).

"Sounds just like something Josh would say," Shannon observed.

"I can't believe he's dead, Melva." Landon began to cry.

"Oh, Landon, he isn't dead. He is alive. He is more alive than he has ever been. He just isn't here."

"What do we do now?" Eric asked.

"What do we do? We prepare for Heaven like Josh did. His entire life was given to God. And since he lived for God on earth, he will live with God in Heaven."

Melva looked at the three children standing in front of her. She thought for a moment about all they had learned together. Lessons God had taught them about growth and peace and love. Stories about the Wemmicks, Punchinello, and the song of the king.

"God used Josh to teach us a lot," she said, pulling Shannon onto her lap and putting her arms around the boys. "We will miss him. But we will see him again. And when we do, we will be together forever. That's what God has promised. And that's no secret."

Life

Probably no topic is avoided more than death. It looms as the final enemy. But on the cross Christ defeated death and Satan. And because of *His* victory, death for the Christian becomes merely a doorway into eternal life.

If we could see through God's eyes, we would see the wonderful things He has in store for us in Heaven—mansions, streets of gold, the Tree of Life, the presence of Jesus!

And Jesus is preparing a place just for you (as well as for your friends, if you invite them). A perfect place, tailor-made, more beautiful than anything you could imagine.

I saved the best for last though. The best part for me is that the One who paid for my entrance is the One who will welcome me in. You'll recognize Him by the nail prints as He beckons you *home*. All of a sudden it won't seem so scary any more.

"Do not let your hearts be troubled. Trust in God; trust also in me. In my Father's house are many rooms; if it were not so, I would have told you. I am going there to prepare a place for you. And if I go and prepare a place for you, I will come back and take you to be with me that you also may be where I am." JOHN 14:1–3 (NIV)

"For to me, to live is Christ and to die is gain." PHILIPPIANS 1:21 (NIV)

"We are confident, I say, and would prefer to be away from the body and at home with the Lord." 2 CORINTHIANS 5:8 (NIV)